**In all honesty
I don't like you and you don't like me
But, I feel that what we have now is working.**

I allow you to live here
and you skitter about,
murdering until your heart is content.

However,

We need to lay out some ground rules
if we want this to become a "long term solution."

Move when I am not around
try to stick to walls.
I have seen Spider-Man
Starring Tobey Maguire, Andrew Garfield, and Tom Holland
and if they taught me anything,
it's that you are pretty adept at this.

Now I know you may be wondering:

"Why must I adhere to these rules
that only dignify me as a second-class citizen?"

Well it's for your protection
Specifically, protection from me.

And I know this may be difficult
But I believe in you
And I know that you will hold true to this agreement.

With that said
I look forward to never seeing you again
Ever!
Have a nice day.

To the Spider In My House

Hey you there!
Yeah you!
I see you!
Sitting there in the corner.

Carefully on guard,
Watching, prepared.

In all honesty,
I don't like you,
and you don't like me
But, I feel that what we have now is
working.

I allow you to live here
and you skitter about,
murdering until your heart is content.

However,

We need to lay out some ground rules
if we want this to become a

"long term solution."

The major rule being,
I don't ever want to see you.
Stay out of my direct line of sight.

Do you understand?

Move when I am not around.
Try to stick to walls.
I feel this should be easy.
I have seen Spider-Man,
Starring Tobey Maguire, Andrew
Garfield, and Tom Holland
and if they have taught me anything
It's that you're pretty adept at this.

Now I know you may be wondering

"Why must I adhere to these rules
That only dignify me as a second
class citizen?"

Well it is for your protection,
Specifically, protection from me.

I am not a murderer
But if I, happen, to open the shower and you're in the bathtub
Messing around

Then I may,
out of instinct
Turn the shower on sending you cascading to your watery death.

Which I know is something that neither of us want.
And I know this may be difficult
But I believe in you
And know that you will hold true to this agreement.

With that said
I look forward to never seeing you again,
Ever!
Have a nice day.

Sincerely,
A very scared human

Bobby's Flying Machine

"This has to work" he says
Wiping the sweat from his brow.
He looks up at the machine he created,
complex and long.

He follows the rope from the floor to the ceiling
through the pulley then back down
and around his waist.

This rope,
attached to a counter weight hoisted
high
off the ground
connected to some thin twine
within scissors
open and poised.

Near the scissors a rubber band laid taught and tight ready to explode forward
when the switch underneath it is flipped by the marble
that gets pushed by the dominoes,
all standing at attention waiting for the call to drop.

All that they need is for the fan to flip on and knock the bouncy ball off the shelf
setting in motion a chain of events,
that together somehow had to work.

Because everyone wants to fly and everyone can
but sometimes you gotta create something crazy enough
just to get your feet off the ground

Thinking Nothing

It is pretty tough to think about nothing.
Try it.

See, even now you're thinking about
Thinking nothing,
Which is something.
Reading this in whatever voice you think works.
Like a little girl
Or big scary monster.

Go back and try the whole thing again
But this time try it like a monster.
I'll wait.

Wild right!?

Leave the Light On

Please leave the light on,

After the sun has disappeared from the sky
And streetlights have all gone out,

After dinner was cooked, eaten, and cleaned up,
When everyone's favorite shows have ended
And the kids were all tucked in and dreaming,

After the dog was walked and the games were over
And every person out there has called it a night,

Please leave the light on
because I promise
I'm coming home.

CPSIA information can be obtained
at www.ICGtesting.com
Printed in the USA
BVHW022234251219
567830BV00005B/222/P